W9-ACT-006

# Ten Black Dots
## Donald Crews

Greenwillow Books, *An Imprint of* HarperCollins*Publishers*

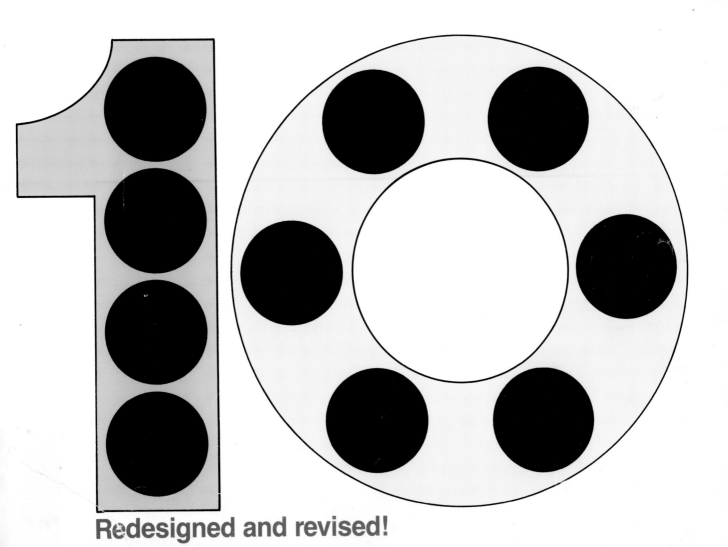

**Redesigned and revised!**

*For Louis*
*whom I just*
*met, and*
*Nina & Amy*
*whom I've*
*known a*
*good while*

The four-color preseparated
art was printed in red,
yellow, blue, and black.
The typeface is Helvetica Bold.

Ten Black Dots
Copyright © 1968, 1986
by Donald Crews
All rights reserved.
Manufactured in China
www.harperchildrens.com
First Edition
22  21  20  19

Library of Congress
Cataloging-in-Publication Data
Crews, Donald.
Ten black dots.
Summary: A counting book
which shows what can be
done with ten black dots—
one can make a sun,
two a fox's eyes, or
eight the wheels of a train.
[1. Counting.
2. Stories in rhyme]
I. Title
II. Title: 10 black dots
PZ8.3.C867Te 1986
[E]    85-14871
ISBN 0-688-06067-6 (trade)
ISBN 0-688-06068-4 (lib. bdg.)
ISBN 0-688-13574-9 (pbk.)

# What can you do with ten black dots?

**1** One dot
can make
a sun

**or a moon
when day
is done.**

**2** Two dots
can make the
eyes of a fox

**or the eyes
of keys that
open locks.**

**3** Three dots
can make a
snowman's face

**or beads
for stringing
on a lace.**

**4 Four dots
can make seeds from
which flowers grow**

**or the
knobs on
a radio.**

**5 Five dots can make buttons on a coat**

**or the
portholes
of a boat.**

**6 Six dots
can make marbles
that you hold—**

**half are
new, the rest
are old.**

**7 Seven dots
can make the spots
on a snake**

**or stones
turned up by a
garden rake.**

**8 Eight dots can make the wheels of a train**

**carrying freight
through sun
and rain.**

**9** Nine dots
can make toy soldiers
standing in rank

**or the pennies
in your
piggy bank.**

**10** Ten dots
can make balloons
stuck in a tree—

**shake the branch
and set
them free.**

Count
them.
Are there
really ten?
Now we
can begin
again,
counting
dots
from one
to ten.

**1**

**2**

**3**

**4**

**5**